4551 6159

WITHDRAWN

The Peace Book

TODD PARR

Megan Tingley Books

LITTLE, BROWN AND COMPANY

Books for Young Readers

New York   Boston

A special note from Todd:
I remember in grade school being excited every year when I got my orange
UNICEF box and went door to door collecting money. I always felt good that
I was making a difference. Growing up in a small town in Wyoming, I never
fully understood how big the world was or the impact one person can have on
someone a world away. I'm proud that a portion of the proceeds from this
book will help UNICEF spread its message of peace to the world.

Little, Brown and Company

Hachette Book Group
237 Park Avenue, New York, NY 10017
Visit our website at www.lb-kids.com

Little, Brown and Company is a division of Hachette Book Group, Inc.
The Little, Brown name and logo are trademarks of Hachette Book Group, Inc.

First Paper Over Board Edition: February 2005
First Paperback Edition: April 2009

Library of Congress Cataloging-in-Publication Data

Parr, Todd.
 The peace book / by Todd Parr.—1st ed.
  p. cm.
 "Megan Tingley Books"
 Summary: Describes peace as making new friends, sharing a meal, feeling good about yourself, and
more.
 ISBN 978-0-316-83531-2 (hc 10x10) / ISBN 978-0-316-05962-6 (hc 9x9) / ISBN 978-0-316-04349-6 (pb)
  [1. Peace—Fiction.] I. Title.
PZ7.P2447Pe 2003
[E]—dc22   2003058914

10 9 8 7 6 5 4 3

PHX

Printed in China

Peace is making new friends

Peace is keeping the water blue
for all the fish

Peace is listening to different kinds of music

Peace is saying you're sorry when you hurt someone

Peace is helping your neighbor

Peace is reading all different kinds of books

Peace is thinking about someone you love

Peace is giving shoes to

someone who needs them

Peace is planting a tree

Peace is sharing a meal

Peace is wearing different clothes

Peace is watching it snow

Peace is keeping the streets clean

Peace is offering a hug
to a friend

Peace is everyone

having a home

Peace is growing a garden

Peace is taking a nap

Peace is learning another language

Peace is having enough pizza in the world for everyone

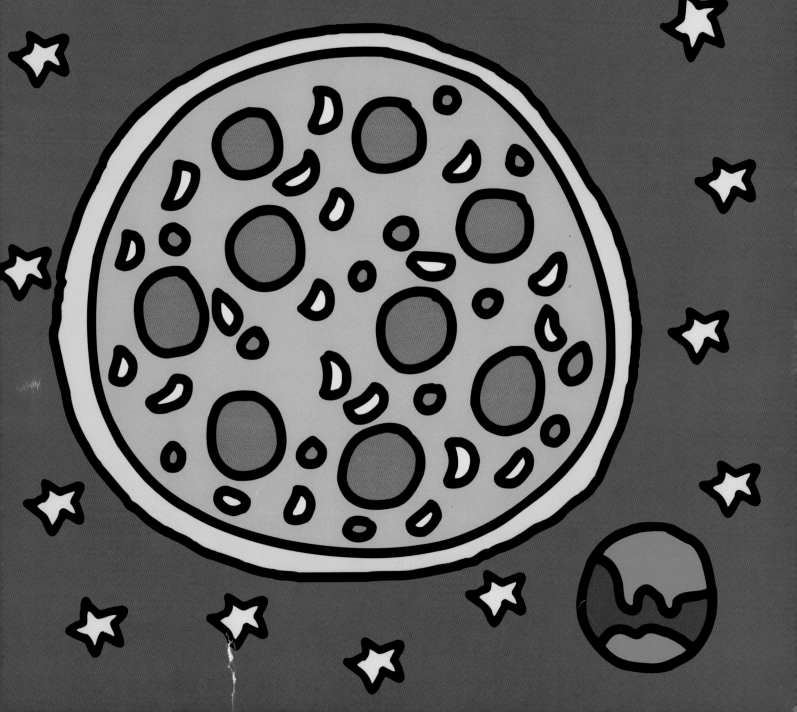

Peace is keeping someone warm

Peace is new babies being born

Peace is being free

Peace is traveling to
different places

Peace is wishing on a star

Peace is being

who you are

PEACE is being
different, feeling
good about yourself,
and helping others.
The world is a
better place because
of YOU!

♡ Love,
Todd